SOME
GOOD NEWS

THE · COBBLE · STREET · COUSINS

SOME
GOOD NEWS

CYNTHIA RYLANT

illustrated by

WENDY ANDERSON HALPERIN

Simon & Schuster Books for Young Readers

SIMON & SCHUSTER BOOKS FOR YOUNG READERS
An imprint of Simon & Schuster Children's Publishing Division
1230 Avenue of the Americas
New York, New York 10020

Book design by Heather Wood
The text of this book is set in Garth Graphic.
The illustrations are rendered in pencil and watercolor.
Printed and bound in the United States of America

1   3   5   7   9   10   8   6   4   2

Library of Congress Cataloging-in-Publication Data
Rylant, Cynthia.
The Cobble Street cousins : some good news / Cynthia Rylant;
illustrated by Wendy Anderson Halperin.
p.   cm.
Summary : Nine-year-old cousins Rosie, Lily, and Tess
make a neighborhood newspaper celebrating all their friends on Cobble Street.
ISBN 0-689-81713-4
[1. Newspapers—Fiction. 2. Cousins—Fiction. 3. Neighborhood—Fiction.]
I. Halperin, Wendy Anderson, ill. II. Title. III. Title: Some good news.
PZ7.R982Cj   1999c   [Fic]—dc21   98-19568   CIP AC

first edition

TABLE OF CONTENTS

For Cousin Katie

C.R.

For Cousins Peter, Teddy,
Andrew, Johnny, and Joel

W.A.H.

SOME
GOOD NEWS

A GREAT IDEA

 *E*arly spring was a beautiful time on Cobble Street. The Japanese cherry trees were all in bloom, tulips sat brightly in boxes, and robins sang everywhere. Lily, Rosie, and Tess loved to open the windows of Aunt Lucy's attic and just listen to the springtime.

The three girls—each nine years old—were living with Aunt Lucy for a year while their parents toured the world with the ballet. Lily and Rosie were sisters, Tess was their cousin, and Aunt Lucy was loved by them all.

Aunt Lucy owned a little flower shop at the corner of Cobble and Plum, and every afternoon after school the cousins stopped by for tea. Aunt Lucy was a lovely young woman with long red hair and freckles, and visiting her shop was one of the cousins' favorite things to do. They loved to say hello to the

customers and offer them tea and cookies as Aunt Lucy put together beautiful bunches of flowers. And because Aunt Lucy's shop was so popular, many people on Cobble Street had become acquainted with Lily, Rosie, and Tess, making the girls feel truly at home.

And it was this feeling of being part of a wonderful neighborhood that made Lily think of an idea.

"I have an idea," Lily said one evening as the cousins played Scrabble in the attic. They were sitting all cozy in the area they called The Playground—a big spot in the middle of the room full of blankets and toys and games.

"I hope it's an idea to end this game," said Tess, "because I am suffering humiliating defeat." (Tess wanted to be a Broadway actress someday, so she liked to say things in a dramatic way.)

6

"I hope it's an idea to make popcorn," said Rosie. "And biscuits."

"*Biscuits?*" said Tess and Lily together.

"I like biscuits," said Rosie. "And popcorn."

Lily and Tess giggled. Rosie always said such charming, funny things. Of the three cousins, she was the most down-to-earth. But she was never boring.

"Actually," said Lily, "I was thinking about all our friends and neighbors and how much we love to see them, and I thought it might be fun to do a Cobble Street newspaper. What do you think?"

"I think it's a *great* idea!" said Tess.

"I love it," said Rosie.

"It would be good for my writing," said Lily (who hoped to be a poet someday). "And I'd actually get something *published*!"

"I could make up recipes," said Rosie, who loved being in the kitchen.

"I could tell jokes," said Tess. "Like they did in vaudeville."

"Good idea!" said Lily.

"What should we call the paper?" asked Rosie.

"Well, it has to have a ring to it," said Lily.

"The Cobble Street Something-or-Other," suggested Tess.

The cousins thought and thought. Elliott, Tess's cat, rubbed his way from one girl's lap to the next as they pondered.

"It has to sound official," said Lily.

"Like the *Times*," said Rosie, "or the *Post* or..."

"The *Courier!*" said Lily.

"The Cobble Street Courier!" exclaimed Tess. "Bravo!"

"I love it," said Rosie.

"All we have to do now is decide what we're going to write about," said Lily.

"And we have to ask Aunt Lucy if we can use her copy machine," said Rosie.

"Oh, she won't mind," Tess said with a grin. "Not if we promise an interview with Michael."

"*Michael!*" Lily said, smiling. "Perfect!"

Michael was Aunt Lucy's boyfriend. He was very kind and sweet to the cousins and they all liked him very much. They hoped he and Aunt Lucy would get married one day.

"Can I do the interview?" asked Rosie, who was especially fond of Michael. He was so quiet and domestic, just like her.

"Sure," said Lily.

"In that case," said Tess, "I get to interview...
who *do* I want to interview?"

"You'll think of someone," said Lily. "The
important thing is that we talk to Aunt Lucy,
find out how many copies we can publish, and
then decide on stories."

"This is so much fun," said Rosie, stroking
Elliott's warm back.

"Just when I thought we were out of good
ideas," grinned Tess.

Lily smiled. "Not with me around!"

SOUP AND COMPANY

*E*ach cousin had her own little "room" in Aunt Lucy's attic, and the following Saturday it was here, separately, where each girl began working on articles for the newspaper. Aunt Lucy generously had offered to make twenty-five copies of the *Courier* for the cousins to pass around the neighborhood. Now it was time for some serious work.

But, of course, thinking of stories for their paper was not work to the cousins at all. Rosie, tucked in her bed behind a beautiful old patch-work quilt, looked through cookbooks and magazines for good recipes (she had something sweet in mind). With her bears and dolls beside her, Rosie felt she could stay in this room forever.

Behind the long, lacy yellow curtains that made her room, Lily had pulled out the small wicker suitcase where she kept her fountain

pen and special papers for writing. She hoped to write a special poem for the paper, a poem everyone would love and remember.

And Tess, sprawled on her bed behind Aunt Lucy's palm-covered screen from Hawaii, was playing an old Peggy Lee album and trying to remember some of those good jokes she'd heard George Burns tell on TV. She grinned ear to ear as she wrote. Beside her, Elliott purred.

But by noon each cousin was missing the others' company, and wondering what Aunt Lucy was doing, and thinking about lunch.

"Who wants soup and crackers?" Lily called through her curtain.

"I do!" answered Tess. "Tomato!"

"Potato!" called Rosie.

"Great-o!" said Lily.

The three girls bounded down to the kitchen, giggling. And there they found Aunt Lucy and Michael.

"Michael!" said the cousins together.

"It is I," he answered with a smile. Michael always had a soft, sleepy look about him, as if he'd just awakened from a nap.

"And how are the Cobble Street cousins?" he asked.

"Super," said Lily.

"Duper," said Tess.

Everyone looked at Rosie.

"Very well, thank you," she said, smiling.

Everyone laughed.

"Rosie, you were supposed to rhyme!" said Tess.

"Well, you took 'duper,'" said Rosie.

Everyone laughed again.

Aunt Lucy pulled Rosie to her side and hugged her. "Do you girls want lunch?" Aunt Lucy asked.

"We were hoping for soup," said Tess.

"*Souper,*" Lily said, giggling.

Aunt Lucy smiled and walked over to the pantry. "There's chicken noodle...," she said.

"That's me!" said Lily.

"Tomato...,"

"Me!" said Tess.

"broccoli...,"

The cousins and Michael all made faces.

"potato...."

"Me!" said Rosie.

"*And* me," added Michael.

Rosie grinned. She knew she and Michael were a lot alike. She would do a good interview with him.

While everyone waited for soup, they all talked of springtime.

"I love seeing the robins," said Aunt Lucy. "Did you know they can travel thousands of miles and still land in the same backyard they left last year?"

"I'm going to do that," said Tess.

"Do what?" asked Lily.

"Travel thousands of miles and always land in Aunt Lucy's backyard."

Aunt Lucy smiled.

"Spring is good because *everything* comes back," said Rosie. "All the little flowers that hid all winter."

"And the leaves on the trees," said Tess.

"And the bugs," said Michael.

"*Ugh.*" The three cousins frowned.

Rosie looked all around Aunt Lucy's wonderful kitchen and into the parlor next door. She looked at the old-fashioned lamp with fringe on the shade and the carved angel above the doorway and the rose-wreath hanging in the hall.

"I love this old house any season at all," said Rosie.

Aunt Lucy patted Rosie's hand.

"And it loves you," she said. "It's a happy house when it's filled with cousins."

Elliott suddenly jumped into the middle of the table.

"And cats!" exclaimed Lily.

She offered Elliott the rest of her soup. Then everyone watched, smiling, as he lapped at the bowl and purred.

Springtime made everyone happy.

NEWS! NEWS!

*T*he cousins worked on their newspaper all week after school, and by Saturday morning they were ready to make copies for the neighborhood. Aunt Lucy had loaned them the old Royal typewriter she had inherited from *her* aunt (Aunt Lindy!), and Lily had taken on the job of typist.

("Good practice for poets," she reminded the cousins.) Tess had done the artwork, Rosie did the lettering, and the *Courier* was finally ready!

The girls stood by Aunt Lucy's copy machine and watched the newspaper roll out.

"It's beautiful!" said Lily.

"Rosie, your headlines look so great," said Tess.

"And look at *your* great jokes!" added Rosie.

When the copying was all finished, the girls borrowed Aunt Lucy's stapler (and Aunt Lucy's desk) and put their very first newspaper together. Aunt Lucy stepped in and looked over their shoulders.

"I love it," she said. "You cousins are amazing."

"Of course," answered Tess with a grin.

Rosie handed Aunt Lucy a newspaper.

"You get the first one," she said.

THE COBBLE Street Courier

☆ NEWS News ☆

Mr. French, owner of French's Market, is now selling birdhouses.

he makes himself/ Inquire at the market (They're beautiful)

Yay

The mail carrier, Miss Larson, has a new puppy named Kipking! She says he likes cottage cheese and grapes!

Another grape, please?

Please be careful of the little maple tree on the corner of Olive and Plum! It's new.

Weather — sunny we hope!

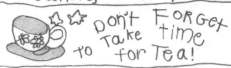

Don't FORGET to take time for Tea!

COBBLE STREET by Lily

I love to live on Cobble Street,
I love the houses so.
The pink one Mrs. White lives in,
The brown ones in a row.
I love the friendly people
And I love the little trees.
I love the cats in windows
And the flowers full of bees.
I love the smell of muffins
Mr. French bakes every day.
I love the little playground
Where the chubby babies play.
The sun shines bright on Cobble Street,
I know it always will.
I love to live on Cobble Street,
Each day is such a thrill.
So please take care of Cobble Street
And keep it clean and bright.
And say a thanks for Cobble Street
When you lie down at night.

LUCY'S FLOWERS FOR YOUR SWEETHEART

An interview with Michael Livingston, who lives in Livingston Arms on Vine.

Q: What is your favorite book?
A: The Borrowers, by Mary Norton.
Q: Why?
A: Because when I was a boy it made me think small and look at small things. I began to notice the tiny things in my backyard especially the different leaves on plants.
Q: Is that why you study botany now?
A: Yes
Q: What is your favorite plant?
A: The Christmas cactus.
Q: Why?
A: Because I think it's a good listener.
Q: Do you sing to your plants?
A: Every day.
Q: What is their favorite song?
A: "Singin' in the Rain"

Thank you Michael
♡→ Rosie
(and Elliott 🐱)

JOKES BY TESS!!

Q: What comes from invisible cows?
A. Evaporated milk!

Q: What instrument can a frog play?
A: A hopsichord!

Q: What's gray and goes squeak, squeak, squeak?
A: An elephant wearing new shoes!

Q: How does a conductor sneeze?
A. Ah Choo-Choo

Rosie's Recipe for Yummy shortbread!

- 4 sticks of soft butter
- 1 cup of sugar
- 4 cups of flour (plus 1/2 cup)

Mix everything together until creamy, then work
in by hand the 1/2 cup of flour.

Press into a round pan (use the bottom of your hand
to press!). Prick nicely with a fork. Sprinkle with sugar.
Bake at 300 degrees for 1 hour.

Cut while warm and serve with cinnamon Tea! Yum!

If you're young like us, you should ask for assistance from an adult!

French's Market for Your apple a Day

★ ★★★★★★★★ ★★★

Here's an idea: Take a clean rag and dip it in blue paint. Blot it all over your white bedroom wall and it will look

Heavenly

Tess interviews ELLIOT (her cat)

Q: Elliott, how do you like living on Cobble Street?
A. Purrfect!

Q: What is your favorite color?
A: Purrple

Q: What do you want to be in your next life?
A: A purrson.

Q: How long do you plan to live with Tess?
A. Purrmanently!

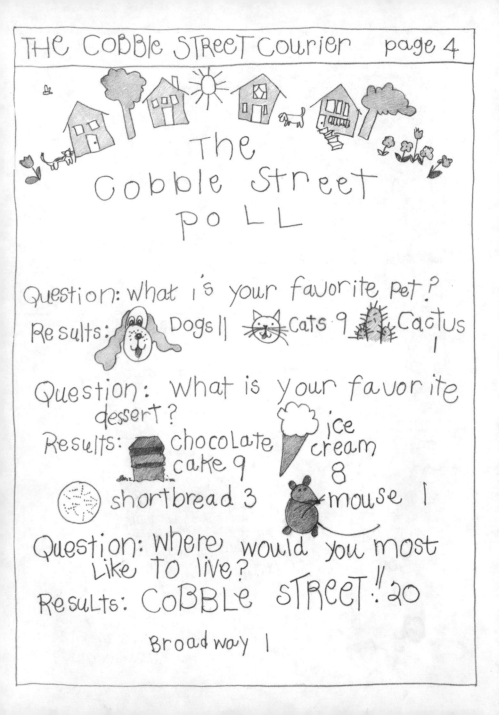

The
Cobble Street
PoLL

Question: what is your favorite pet?
Results: Dogs 11   Cats 9   Cactus 1

Question: what is your favorite dessert?
Results: chocolate cake 9   ice cream 8
shortbread 3   mouse 1

Question: where would you most like to live?
Results: CoBBLe STReeT! 20

Broadway 1

"Now let's deliver!" said Lily.

And the cousins did just that.

Y A R D L E Y

*E*veryone *loves* it!" Tess said excitedly as the three cousins ran up to the attic with the last copy of the *Courier* they had left. All the rest they'd given out at Aunt Lucy's shop and at French's Market.

"I can't believe Mr. French gave us a free birdhouse!" said Rosie, lifting it out of the paper bag she was carrying. It was shaped like a star and painted in yellow and blue stripes.

"Aunt Lucy will love it," said Lily. "We should hang it on the front porch for her."

Tess picked up Elliott and plopped down on a pillow in The Playground.

"I never knew publishing was so fun," she said. "I could have told a *million* more jokes."

"I think Michael liked the interview," said Rosie. "He said that no one had ever asked him about singing to his plants before."

"You know what we forgot to do?" asked Lily. "We forgot to take a copy to Mrs. White!"

"Oh, my goodness," said Rosie.

"We have to give her this last copy," said Tess. "She'll love being in Lily's poem. We should run right over."

"Maybe Michael will come with us," said Rosie. "He likes Mrs. White."

"Rosie, you always want Michael to come with us," said Lily. "But he has to study. He's getting a *Ph.D*!"

"A Pretty Hard Degree," said Tess.

"Well, let's just call him and see," said Rosie. "We could have such a nice tea all together with Mrs. White."

So the cousins phoned Michael.

"I'd love to come with you," he said. "But I have to bring Yardley."

"Who's Yardley?" asked Rosie.

"My father's basset hound," answered Michael. "I'm baby-sitting."

"*Perfect!*" cried the cousins.

And they combed their hair and hurried over to Vine Street.

Michael was waiting for them in front of his apartment building with a sweet, fat, adorable basset hound at his feet.

"*Oh!*" cried all three cousins, dropping to their knees to pet and kiss the friendly dog.

"Yardley loves attention," said Michael. "It's his favorite thing next to pizza."

"He eats *pizza?*" said Tess.

"My father can't help himself," said Michael.

"He gives Yardley pizza, corn chips, Swiss cheese...."

"It shows," smiled Rosie, patting Yardley's tummy as he rolled over for her. "But Yardley is beautiful, anyway."

"He even sleeps with my father," said Michael. "Sometimes with his head on the pillow!"

Lily smiled at Michael.

"Your dad sounds great," she said. "You should bring him to see us at Aunt Lucy's."

Michael reached over to straighten Yardley's collar.

"I will," he said. "Maybe when your parents come back from their tour. We could have sort of a reunion or a ... a ... "

"A *wedding!*" said Tess.

Lily gasped and covered Tess's mouth with her hand. Rosie giggled. And Michael blushed a deep scarlet around his collar.

"Well ...." He smiled. "I ... *yikes.*"

Everyone looked at each other, then burst into laughter.

"We'd better get going!" said Lily. "Before Tess finishes any more sentences!"

So the cousins and Michael strolled over to
Mrs. White's little pink house, retelling Tess's
funny vaudeville jokes and reciting lines from
Lily's poem. And Yardley lumbered happily
along beside them.

A SMALL WORLD

$\mathcal{M}$rs. White was delighted to see everyone. Because she was ninety years old, she didn't get out to do much visiting herself. So she was always happy for company. *Especially* when the company was cousins.

"Girls!" said Mrs. White at the door of her small pink house. "And Michael! How nice to see all of you! And who is *this*? She smiled, looking at Yardley. Yardley wagged his tail and licked her hand.

"This is my father's dog, Yardley," said Michael. "He'll wait for us in the backyard. I hope you don't mind my bringing him."

"Of course not," said Mrs. White. "He's a sweetheart."

"We brought you a copy of our first newspaper, Mrs. White," said Lily.

"It's called *The Cobble Street Courier*," Tess said.

"I interviewed Michael," Rosie added with a grin, poking Michael's arm.

"Oh, wonderful, wonderful," said Mrs. White. "How lovely. Do come in and visit."

Michael let Yardley into Mrs. White's backyard, then everyone stepped inside her parlor.

Tess held up a small bag.

"We stopped at French's Market and got some fresh olive bread, Mrs. White. And some cream cheese."

"And sparkling apple cider in a fancy bottle," said Lily. "We thought we'd toast our success with you."

"Wonderful!" said Mrs. White. "Let me get some dishes."

"Oh, no," said Michael. "We don't want to make a mess in your kitchen. Rosie was smart enough to remember paper plates and cups."

"With kittens on them," Rosie said with a grin. Mrs. White loved cats. She even made tiny cat dolls.

"Well, then, let me add some nice strawberries to the party," said Mrs. White. "My neighbor Mr. Harrison just dropped by with some."

"Should we invite him?" asked Michael.

"Well," said Mrs. White, "I'm sure he'd like that. He's a widower with no family and doesn't see many people. Are you sure you wouldn't mind?"

"Of course not!" said the three cousins.

"I'll phone him," Mrs. White said, smiling.

Before long, the cousins, Michael, Mrs. White, and Mr. Harrison were all seated at Mrs. White's small dining room table in front of the picture window. Mr. Harrison was a little shy, Lily could see, so she made a special effort to be nice to him.

"Do you have a garden, Mr. Harrison?" she asked.

He smiled.

"Indeed I do. Every summer I have so many tomatoes, I have to give them away to everyone on the street."

"I love fresh tomatoes," said Michael.

"Michael is studying to be a botanist," Lily told Mr. Harrison.

"How nice," said the elderly man. "What a wonderful way to spend one's life, studying plants."

Michael smiled.

He liked Mr. Harrison already.

"I want to spend my life singing," said Tess.

"I want to spend mine writing," said Lily.

Everyone looked at Rosie.

"I want cats," said Rosie.

They all laughed.

"That sounds best of all, Rosie," said Mr. Harrison.

Rosie grinned proudly.

"What sort of work have you done in your life, Mr. Harrison?" asked Michael.

"Oh, I've done several things," answered Mr. Harrison. "I was a teacher. Then a lawyer. Finally—"

"A senator," finished Mrs. White with a proud smile on her face.

"Oh, my goodness," said Rosie.

"He was a state senator for twenty-five years," said Mrs. White. "And a good one."

"Then you must have known my grand-father," said Michael.

"Yes?" asked Mr. Harrison.

"His name was Charles Livingston. He was..."

"A federal court judge!" said Mr. Harrison. "I certainly did know him! A fine man. Very intelligent."

"It is a small world," said Mrs. White.

51

"Gosh, we already have a great story for our next paper," said Tess. "Could I interview you sometime, Senator Harrison?"

"I'd be honored," he said, smiling.

Suddenly everyone heard a scratching at the back door. Then a whine. Then a bark like a bass drum.

Michael smiled.

"Yardley knows we have cream cheese," he said. "And he wonders why he isn't getting his share."

Rosie giggled.

"He ain't nothin' but a hound dog," she said.

"Well." Mrs. White smiled. "Let's let the poor dear in. I don't mind. Truly. I like dogs."

"You're sure?" asked Michael.

"I'm sure," said Mrs. White.

So Yardley joined everyone at the table,
wagging his tail, sniffing shoes, putting a paw
on Michael's knee.

"Maybe we'll interview Yardley for our next
issue," said Lily, letting the dog lick some
cream cheese from her fingers.

"I know what *Yardley* will want to be in *his* next life," said Tess.

"What?" asked Michael.

"A *chef*!"

Everyone laughed and laughed.

It had been a wonderful week for the three young cousins on Cobble Street.

And there would be more wonderful weeks to come!